# MIA CLARK

ISBN: 1511530022
ISBN-13: 978-1511530026

*Book design by Cerys du Lys*
*Cover design by Cerys du Lys*
*Cover Image © Depositphotos | avgustino*

Cherrylily.com

# DEDICATION

Thank you to Ethan and Cerys for helping me with this book and everything involved in the process. This is a dream come true and I wouldn't have been able to do it without them. Thank you, thank you!

# CONTENTS

# ACKNOWLEDGMENTS

Thank you for taking a chance on my book!

I know that the stepbrother theme can be a difficult one to deal with for a lot of people for a variety of reasons, and so I took that into consideration when I was writing this. While this is a story about forbidden love, it's also a story about two people becoming friends, too. Sometimes you need someone to push you in your life, even when you think everything is fine. Sometimes you need someone to be there, even when you don't know how to ask them to stay with you.

This is that kind of story. It is about two people becoming friends, and then becoming lovers. The forbidden aspects add tension, but it's more than that, too. Sometimes opposites attract in the best way possible. I hope you enjoy my books!

# STEPBROTHER WITH BENEFITS

## Introduction

HOW DID I WIND UP NAKED, face down ass up on my bed, with my stepbrother behind me, thrusting hard into me, my face buried in a pillow to muffle my moans while our parents are downstairs making dinner and waiting for us to join them so we can eat? Well, that's a long story. To be honest, I'm not even sure how this started. It's so wrong, and I know we shouldn't be doing this, but then why does it feel so good? Why do I love it? Why am I...

I think I love it a little too much. I'm even starting to worry myself.

He leans over me and pins me to the bed, burying himself deep inside of me with one last thrust. I know what's coming next, but I can barely think anymore. My body's already betrayed me and given in to the delicious feeling of his thick, hard cock inside me. I've never had orgasms as powerful as the ones I have with Ethan, and this current climax is one of my stronger ones. My pussy milks his cock, my inner walls clenching against him as he cums inside of me.

I feel it, and it feels so perfect, so warm and soft despite the fact that he was just fucking me hard. I don't understand anything about Ethan. I don't know how he can be like this. He's some kind of walking contradiction. I don't know why we're in bed together.

I don't want to ever leave, though.

He stays inside of me, jet after jet of his cum filling me to the brim. I can feel it seeping out of me, just a little. It's going to leave a mess on my bed. I don't know how I'm supposed to explain this.

I just want to lay here, just a little longer, I want to stay here with him inside of me. I want to...

I want to lay back and cuddle with him and...

No. That's not part of our arrangement. We can't do that. My God, he's my brother! Step-brother, I remind myself. But still.

He pulls out of me and slaps me on the ass.

"Let's go, Princess. Mom and Dad are waiting," Ethan says, cocky and confident as ever.

"I can't believe we did that," I say in disbelief. I laugh, but he just smirks at me.

"You know you loved it," he says, reaching for his pants on the floor.

There's something about the way he says it, something about how casual it sounds, but I feel like there's more to his words, too. I don't know why I feel like that, because this is Ethan we're talking about. He's a bad boy, and everyone knows it. No one and nothing can tame him. He does what he wants, when he wants. I didn't just love it, I love...

Stop, Ashley. Don't do this to yourself.

I thought I'd learned to deal with it. I mean, our parents have been married for three years already, so I should have figured him out by now, right? Nope, not really.

I lay on the bed and watch him put his pants on. They're loose around his waist and hang from his hips, even after he's zipped and buttoned them up. Ethan plays football in college--he even has a scholarship, though it's not like he needs it since his dad is rich--and he's got muscles in all the right places. That slick, perfect V angling from his hips to his crotch.

It's like an arrow pointing to everything I want. Or a warning sign telling me to run away because this is dangerous. Maybe Ethan's bad boy personality is rubbing off on me. I've been feeling really naughty lately, so I wouldn't be surprised.

I'm still naked from the waist down when he finishes putting his clothes back on. He stares at me, giving me a weird, confusing kind of look. Ethan walks back to the bed, leans over me, and without saying anything or even asking, he thrusts two fingers deep into my sex.

I gasp and my back arches before I can think or do or say anything. Somehow I manage to breathe out his name. "Ethan!"

"Listen, Ashley, you think you can get away with looking at me like that, laying on your bed with no pants on? Nah, I don't think so. You're still mine right now. Yeah, that's a good girl. Fuck, you're so sensitive. How many orgasms did you have? Tell me."

I whimper and beg him with little muttered words, but he ignores me.

"Tell me. Now. How many?"

"Four," I say, a whisper.

"Louder," Ethan says.

"Mom and Dad will... they'll hear us, Ethan. You need to stop."

"You think I care?"

It sounds harsh, but there's a subtle softness in his eyes. Ethan wouldn't hurt me, he wouldn't be mean to me. I don't expect you to understand, but it's a part of this, it's one of the rules we made together. The rules that we don't seem to be following anymore, since we were supposed to stop this when our parents came back...

"Tell me how many orgasms you had?" he asks me again. "Your pussy is mine, and I want you to keep track."

"Four," I say again, louder, but now it's a lie. "Five," I say, correcting myself, blushing.

My body spasms on the bed as my brother fingerfucks me, pushing past the grip of my orgasm, making me whimper and writhe in ecstatic release.

When he's done, when I'm finished, he pulls his fingers out of me and shoves them in my mouth. "Taste," he says.

I open my mouth without thinking and lick around his fingers, sucking them like they're his cock. I open my eyes and peek towards his crotch and notice that, yes, he's erect again. I really could be sucking his cock. Maybe I will. Maybe...

"Now put some damn pants on," he says, smiling, teasing me. "Mom and Dad are waiting for us."

Mia Clark

# 1 - Ashley

*(Four Days Earlier)*

T HIS ISN'T GOING TO WORK."

"Huh?" I ask.

"Ashley, this isn't going to work. Have you thought about how we're going to do this? We're leaving for summer break. Right now. You're going back to your parents and I'm going back to mine. How are we going to do this?"

"Jake, I don't know what you're talking about."

And, I don't. I really don't, especially considering we just had sex. Literally. We're in Jake's dorm room while his roommate is out, and one thing led to another, and, well...

I don't usually do this. I don't want Jake to think I'm a... a slut or anything. We've only had sex once before, but I thought that since we were going back home for summer break, this was a good time to do it again. I won't be able to see him for a few months.

"Ash, you live five hours away from me. We'll be apart the whole summer. What kind of relationship is that?"

"Um... a long distance one?" I say.

He laughs, but it's not a nice laugh. Kind of a douchebag asshole laugh, actually. Which is really mean considering he just had his dick inside me. The least he could do is be a little nicer.

I can't believe I'm even thinking this. Nicer? Yeah, Ashley, um... he's your boyfriend! He *should* be nice to you. Duh?

"I don't do long distance relationships, babe," Jake says. "It's not my thing."

"So you're breaking up with me?" I ask, as if I couldn't say anything stupider at the moment.

Yes, I've got perfect grades, I was the top of my class in high school, and I've got three scholarships that will more than cover most of my first two years of college, but apparently I'm still dumb enough to have to ask if my boyfriend is breaking up with me.

"I'm not breaking up with you," he says.

"Oh," I say. He makes no sense to me.

"I'm just saying we can't do this. I can't go the entire summer without sex, babe. It's impossible."

"Oh." I have no idea where he's going with this.

"We'll take a break. See other people. At least for the summer. When we get back to school next year we can pick up where we left off."

"Wait..."

Look, I know what you're thinking. I'm not an idiot, alright? I'm really not. I just... I like Jake. I think. I'm not sure how I feel about him. I'd never had a boyfriend before college, and even then my boyfriends up until now haven't exactly been... boyfriends? I dated a couple of guys for a week or two, but that's it. Jake and I have been going out for a couple months now and I thought everything was going well, but...

Nope, apparently not.

"It's not you, it's me," he says.

"Yeah, obviously," I say. I know it's not me. What a stupid thing to say. He's the one breaking up with me!

Jake laughs. "It'll be fine. Go home and have a few one night stands or something. Learn how to be better in bed. You're kind of stiff, you know? You need to get a little more into it. When we come back to school next year, we can date again. Trial run or something? See how it goes. I've been putting up with you for now, but I really need someone who knows what they're doing, Ash. The sex just hasn't been that good. Sorry to put it out there like that."

"No," I say. "It's fine."

That's not what I want to say. I want to say more. I want to say something witty and funny and sarcastic. Because I don't think it's me. He's not very good in bed, either. Selfish and fast is about how I'd explain it, but I thought he liked me, so...

My God, I'm an idiot, aren't I?

I put my clothes on and rush to the door just as his roommate is coming back. His roommate accidentally blocks me from making a hasty retreat until we shuffle around to either side and I can get past him. I want to go. I want to run back to my room and pack and leave right now, because... because...

Jake is an asshole! I almost think about screaming it, but I stop myself. I can't do that. I'm the good girl, the girl with perfect grades, the girl everyone expects to go far in life. I'm...

I'm a doormat, apparently. I'm the girl whose boyfriend breaks up with her so he can sleep with other women during a two month summer break from college. Wow.

Really, wow.

"Text me sometime or something," Jake yells to me as I rush down the hall.

"Fuck you," I say. I want to shout it, but I don't. I whisper it to myself under my breath.

I'm Ashley Banks and I'm a good girl. Good girls don't swear and shout down the halls. I can't do that, even if I want to.

# 2 - Ethan

T HE SCHOOL YEAR'S OVER. I'm supposed to be packing up to leave. Supposed to be, but yeah, guess what I'm doing instead? Something stupid.

A couple of guys from the team dragged me out to play shirts versus skins football on the field because the cheerleaders were doing some last hoorah celebration, complete with those fuckably short skirts they love to wear. Fuck. Those legs. That ass. Fuck. Just fuck.

I can't deal with this shit, man. You don't even know how fucking hard this is right now.

Shirts versus skins, but it devolved into skins versus skins soon enough. Who even gives a fuck what team we're on? No one, apparently. It's all some ruse to impress the cheerleaders, so it's not like it matters. And, yeah, it's working. They're doing their little cheer celebration, but they keep looking over at us. Can't say I blame them.

This is college football and we're in the prime of our lives. Look, I'm kind of an asshole, alright? I know it. Everyone knows it. No reason to hide it.

I look good, though. Especially with a shirt off. Especially when I'm sweating, muscles tight, running around a field, throwing a football.

What position? Quarterback. Shouldn't it be obvious? I was born to be in the spotlight.

Probably helps that my dad's rich. Can't hurt at least.

The cheerleaders are done, and now they're just sitting on the bleachers watching us. Some of the guys pretend to have a huddle or some stupid shit, but it's all of them together. No offense, but what the fuck kind of huddle is that? Two teams would never huddle together. Doesn't make any goddamn sense.

"Last play, guys," someone says. "Make it good. Flashy. Then let's go get our water bottles. Make that flashy, too."

I almost laugh. *These guys*. They really need to get laid. I guess they're about to, so it's all good.

I do some flashy shit, throw the ball higher in the air than necessary so it looks cooler when someone catches it. I don't even care who, just someone. It works. They do. Is that guy supposed to be on my team? I can't tell anymore.

Stupid. This isn't real football, it's just stupid.

We're done. It's over. Walking. Yup.

You might be asking how someone drinks water from a water bottle in a flashy way. And if you're asking that, you need to stop and calm down a little because it's about to happen, so just sit there and see for yourself.

We all go get our water. I drink mine, because I'm thirsty, and not the kind of *thirsty* that these guys are. Yeah, the cheerleaders are cute, but I don't need or want any of that pussy right now. They don't do much for me. I'm a bad boy, but I've still got standards, you know?

The rest of the guys get real into it, though. Drinking, but losing half the water, letting it splash down their faces, dripping past their throats, onto their bare chests. Dude, you're already sweaty from football, so I don't know what this is going to do.

Whatever. It works. Fucking A, it works. It's like cheerleader bait or some shit. They flock to the muscled meat in front of them. Solo, in pairs, or sometimes three at a time, each heading towards the man of their dreams.

Dreams. Ha! Yeah, right. You know how long dreams last? One night. Then you forget about them when you wake up in the morning. This is pretty much the same thing, but it'll be even shorter. We're all leaving this afternoon and going back home.

Home.

A bunch of cheerleaders flock towards me, even though I didn't put on a show for them. Five. More than the other guys. I briefly wonder if I could have them all at the same time. Greedy, much? What the fuck would I even do with five girls at once? I don't know, but I wouldn't mind finding out sometime. I've got two hands, a cock, and a mouth. I'm sure the last girl can think of something to do, too. It'll work.

"Hey, Ethan."

"Hey, Chelsea," I say.

"Hey, Ethan."

This goes on. And on. Five times. Fuck my life.

Chelsea, Jaime, Robin, Maxi, and Bella. I'm not that much of a dick, alright? I do know what their names are. I've talked to them before. I'm on the football team and they're cheerleaders. Get off my case.

Yes, fuck you, I slept with Bella. That's it. Just her. Alright, look, shut the fuck up, I made out with Chelsea and Robin at the same time, and maybe I fingered Jaime, and, yes, I let Maxi suck my cock, but that's it.

Don't fucking judge me.

"Look, this is real interesting," I say, even though they've been babbling on for five minutes and I don't remember a word of what they said. "I've got to go, though. Plane to catch."

"Awww."

"Awww."

Five of those. Fuck my life. Seriously, just fuck it.

"I'll see you next year, though. Good job uh... cheering?"

They actually do a good job, so it's not like this is a stretch, but it sounds goofy as fuck. They act like it's the nicest compliment anyone's ever given them, though.

"Thanks, Ethan!"

You know the drill. Five of those. Wow, seriously?

"Talk to you ladies later," I say.

I think that's it. Or I thought that was it, but when I start to walk away, I've got a following. Yeah, you guessed it, five.

"Do you need help packing?" Chelsea asks.

"Back in your room?" Maxi adds.

"We don't mind." That's Robin.

"If we help you pack fast..." Jaime.

Bella's not even subtle. She mimes sucking my cock by poking her tongue in her cheek and moving her hand in front of her mouth when she thinks no one else is looking. The other girls giggle when they see her.

I don't even fucking know what is going on anymore. Is this real life? Fuck.

"I'm done packing," I lie. "Have to leave now, actually. Seriously, my plane's leaving in an hour. I'm going to be late." Another lie, I've got four hours and the plane isn't going to leave without me.

Did I mention my dad's rich? Private company jet. You have no idea how good that shit is. Seriously, it's good.

They all make a sad little pouty face, but I just laugh and keep on walking. I notice some of the other guys nearby staring at me like I'm insane.

Hey, fuck you, I'm not insane. I'm Ethan Colton, cocky asshole, arrogant prick, and bad boy extraordinaire. I could fuck every girl here if I wanted to, but it's getting kind of old. I need a change of pace.

# 3 - *Ashley*

'M HOME. I'm here. It's exactly like I remembered it, which is to say it still doesn't feel like home to me.

My mom remarried when I was fifteen, and my stepfather is... well, let's just say he has a lot of money. Colton Enterprises ring a bell? He's basically a billionaire. I like him, but I'm still adjusting, I guess. I try to think of him as a father, and I try to think of this place as my home, but it's still hard.

It doesn't help that overnight I went from being an only child to having a brother, either. It especially doesn't help that my brother is Ethan Colton.

He's a troublemaker. He's always been a troublemaker. I've known him since the second grade, and I don't know if he's changed at all since then. He used to flip up girl's skirts when we were in elementary school, and to be honest he's basically done the same thing ever since. For a different reason now, but it's still all the same to me.

He's the boy your mother warned you about, except my mother never warned me about this. We had "the talk" before she and my stepfather finally married and moved in together, bringing me with her, but it was basically that I'd have a brother now, and she knew it would take some adjusting, but she thought it'd be good for all of us.

Nothing good comes from Ethan, trust me. He's a jerk, a womanizer, a misogynistic prick, he's...

He's standing on the pool deck right now, covered in water, the slick shine of wet sunlight shimmering across his body. I stop and stare, mouth dropped open, still shouldering my packed bag from the trip back here.

He must have just gotten out of the pool, because water is dripping from his board shorts, pooling at his feet. He's hot. I mean, it's hot out. That's what I meant. Please don't put words in my mouth.

This is different, though. Yes, I know my stepbrother is attractive, because how couldn't I? That doesn't make him any less of an arrogant jerk, though. It doesn't mean he's humped and dumped any less woman than he has. It doesn't mean that he's ever had a stable relationship that lasted more than a couple of weeks.

It's just... this is a weird thought to have, and I know it, but it feels like he's just oozing sex right now. Like it's melting off his body, the water acting as a release for his inner sexual beast. Is that...?

No. No! I shouldn't be looking at him that way, this is so disturbing and wrong, but his swim trunks are loose and there's a definite bulge in the front. I don't even want to know what he's thinking about. Is there a girl here? Is he going to... while I'm... ick.

Ethan is an asshole. I don't care if he's hot. Outside, I mean. Swimming. It *is* hot out. Maybe I should go swimming, too? I think my bathing suit still fits me.

While I'm lost in Lala-land, I don't even notice Ethan drying off, wrapping a towel around his waist, and coming back inside. I'm standing there, mouth open, staring at where he used to be, and now he's just smirking at me like it's the most amusing thing he's ever seen.

"Hey, sis," he says. "What's up? Need help with that bag?"

I snap out of it and look away from him. It's cooler inside from the air conditioning, and his skin prickles with goosebumps, his bare chest rippling with hot, chilled muscle, his nipples peaking and hardening. He's just another boy, I remind myself. There's plenty like him, Ashley. You've seen shirtless boy's before.

It's different this time, though. He looks different. I haven't seen Ethan since Christmas break, and it feels like he's changed. Not in a good way, I'm sure.

"Shut up," I tell him. "What are you even doing here?"

"Uh, summer break?" he says. "Should be obvious. Same reason you're here."

"I thought you were going on some vacation or something," I say. "Cancun or whatever? Who knows with you."

"Wow, that hurts," he says, covering his heart with both hands as if I've mortally wounded him. He staggers side to side, acting out this fake death scene. "My own sister, my own flesh and blood, I can't believe this."

"Obviously you haven't taken any biology classes at that party school of yours," I say. "Just because your father married my mother doesn't make us related, especially not by blood, you idiot."

"Ah, yeah, right," he says, flashing me his patented bad boy grin.

I can see why a lot of girls fall for it. Not me, of course. I'm different. I'm only different because I know him better than anyone, probably. It's really not helping right now, though, especially since he's still shirtless. It's doubly not helping with that towel wrapped around his waist. If I didn't just see him standing out there by the pool, I could almost imagine him having just stepped out of the shower, with nothing besides a towel covering his bare body. The remembered image of the slight bulge from before comes back to me, and I have to shake my head in disgust and look away again to stop myself from...

From what? Daydreaming? About Ethan? Ugh! Disgusting.

"Anyways," he says. "Yeah, about summer break. I'm just going to chill here. Maybe we can do some bonding or something. Hang out? Who knows. Unless you're going to be busy doing summer reading or whatever the hell you smart girls do. Write some book report for extra credit next year?"

"Ha ha," I say, faking a laugh. "Right. Funny, Ethan. I don't think we've had to do that since middle school. Not that you'd remember, since you never did it anyways."

"Oh, you're keeping tabs on me now? Cool. I didn't know I was so important to you."

I blush and turn away from him. Again. God, how many times is this going to happen? I can't even look him in the face anymore. I try to tell myself it's because he looks obscene right now, that it's because he's just trying to mess with me, what with being shirtless and vaguely flirting. Is... wait, is that what he's doing? Flirting?

No, definitely not. Not only is he my stepbrother, but I'm not the type of girl someone like Ethan Colton would ever flirt with. He likes the dumb cheerleader type that he can hook up with and then toss aside without much trouble.

He's not stupid. Or, he's got some street smarts. Not the good kind, mind you, but the kind that lets him manipulate and use people.

Not me. I'm not going to fall for his tricks. Never.

"Where are mom and dad?" I ask. "I need to talk to them."

"Gonna have to wait, Princess. They're on vacation for the week."

Since I'm already turned away, and I'm trying to keep myself from stammering and staring at him, I head to the kitchen to get something to drink. Unfortunately Ethan follows me, and now he's closer than ever. I reach into the cabinet to grab a glass and he just reaches up right behind me to get one for himself, too.

He's standing so close to me that our hands brush as we pull the glasses from the cabinet. He's standing so close that I can feel him behind me. Close. So close that...

Holy shit! Oh my God. Yes, that's the bulge. From before. Touching me. Pressing lightly against my butt.

I drop my glass. It starts to fall, heading on a crash course to an imminent, shattering demise. Ethan catches it, though. In the process, he gets even closer to me. Our bodies touch, my back to his front, closer than... closer than I've ever been to someone, almost. Or, not really. I mean, I've had sex before, but that's the closest, and... Ethan is basically as close as that, his erection pressing into... against...

He puts the glasses on the counter and places his hands on my hips. "Hey, Little Miss Perfect, you alright? You're shaking."

I need to make something up, so I say the first thing that comes to mind. "Why didn't they tell me they were going on vacation?"

He's still holding me. Reassuring me? This is weird. But kind of nice. I lean back in his arms and he puts his chin on my shoulder, hands moving towards my stomach. It's weird. Too intimate. It's exactly the sort of thing Ethan would do to rile me up. I can't let him know it bothers me.

It doesn't help that it doesn't bother me. It doesn't help that no one has ever held me this way. Maybe my mom did when I was younger, but that's entirely different. Jake never did, and none of the other boys I dated would have ever thought about it. Especially not after...

I don't want to think about it. I can't believe he broke up with me like that.

"Was a last minute thing," Ethan says close to my ear. "They left a note, told me to tell you. It's just you and me for a week. Hope you can handle it. Don't worry, I'm a good babysitter."

Babysitter? I laugh, harsh, and slap his hands away from my stomach. He was almost hugging me just then, almost holding me in some intimate, tight embrace, but that's just to screw with me. He doesn't care. He's an asshole.

"I don't need a babysitter," I tell him. "Especially not you, Ethan. Besides the fact that I'm an adult now, you wouldn't even know where to begin with a baby."

"Nah, you're wrong, Princess. It's like this. When a man loves a woman, well..." He makes some obscene gesture, touching the index finger of his left hand to his thumb to make an O-shape, then poking his middle and index finger from his left hand through that, simulating sex. Or fingerfucking someone. I wouldn't be surprised if it's both. Why two fingers? That's just gross. He's gross. My God, he's my brother.

Stepbrother, I remind myself. I don't know whether this makes it better or worse.

"Yeah, you do look grown up now, though," he says out of the blue. "Looks nice. I remember you from second grade, with those ugly glasses and those atrocious outfits you used to wear. You've matured well, Princess."

"Stop calling me that," I say. "I'm not your princess, Ethan. And what do you know about how I looked in second grade?"

"Hey, I know a lot about how you looked," he says. "You're the only girl who kept wearing skirts even though I made it my mission during recess to go around flipping up as many girl's skirts as I could."

I slap him. Hard. It's supposed to hurt. It's supposed to be mean and intrusive and punitive, but he just stands there and grins at me with the red print of my palm on his cheek. I go to slap him again, but this time he catches my hand.

"What's wrong?" he asks, giving me this intense look that I don't know what to do with.

"What do you mean what's wrong?" I say, shocked. "Can't you tell? You're being a dick!"

"Whoa, harsh words there, Smarty Pants. I remember when you were too shy to even try to swear. You'd stammer and blush and--"

"Jake broke up with me," I say suddenly and almost without thinking. No, I did think about this, though. It's what I wanted to talk with my mom about. And maybe Ethan's dad. My stepdad. I just... I don't understand. I'm not sure what I'm supposed to do.

"Wait, what? Seriously?" Ethan says. He sounds a lot more sympathetic than I would have given him credit for. "What happened?"

It all comes out. All of it. I haven't been able to talk with anyone about this since I left, not even my friends. I don't have a lot of friends at college anyways. I'm too smart. I know that sounds like it should be a good thing, but I got into a really good school with a ton of scholarships and...

My friends didn't. My old friends, I mean. I never had a lot of them, either. I thought it would be fine, that I could start over, but so far it hasn't worked. I've dated, and I thought everything was going well with Jake, but...

"He just said he can't do it," I say. "He told me he can't go the entire summer without sex, so we needed to break up, but if I wanted to we can get back together at the beginning of next year."

"No fucking way," Ethan says. "He actually said that?"

A crash of tears rushes down my cheeks. I didn't even realize I was crying. I can't say anymore, so I just gulp and nod.

# 4 - Ethan

HOLY FUCKING SHIT. I just want to punch that nerd boyfriend of hers. Yeah, Ashley goes to some preppy school for smart people, whatever. I don't hold it against her. But who does that stupid fuck think he is breaking up with her like that?

Look, I'm an asshole, but I'm not that much of an asshole. I have standards. I'd never date some girl and then dump her like that. I'd probably never date her to begin with, to be honest. A couple weeks, maybe, then a booty call at best, but I try to make it pretty fucking clear what's going on.

It's just fucking, you know? I give you a good time, you give me a good time, then we go our separate ways. Easy.

Jake. What a pussy-ass name, too. I was just teasing her before, but I wrap my arms around her again and hug her. She looks lost. Fuck, her eyes. Ashley has the biggest, brightest brown eyes you've ever seen. Gorgeous, really. They used to be hard to see with her glasses, but when her mom married my dad, he got her LASIK surgery for her sixteenth birthday and ever since then, well...

Yeah, she's got nice eyes. They're the kind of eyes you want looking up at you when you get a blowjob. A little coy, kind of cute, except she's got your cock in her mouth, so that kind of shoves the coy cuteness out the window, now doesn't it?

She's crying right now, though. Fucking ass-hole. Can't even believe he'd do that. I hold her and hug her and we rock back and forth. She's into it, crying against my chest. Maybe I should have put a shirt on when I came inside from the pool, but I didn't expect to stay in here that long. I just wanted to grab something to drink.

"Hey," I say to her. "He's just a stupid fucking prick, alright? Don't even think about him any-more."

She looks up at me. Close. Shit. We're really close, aren't we? Chest to chest. Her bottom lip quivers. I kind of want to suck it between my teeth and nibble on it, then kiss the fuck out of her. Shit, this is Ashley, she's my sister.

Stepsister, I remind myself. But what the hell difference does it make? It's the same thing, same idea. I've known this girl since second grade.

I remember thinking she used to wear the cutest panties for a dork. I didn't know what to call it at the time, but if I had to put words to it now, I would have thought she was a lady on the streets and a freak in the sheets. Nice, huh? Yeah, even my second grade self was an asshole and a sex fiend. No one's ever complained about the latter. I take care of the girls I'm with.

I bet Jake's some limp dick fuck who can't even satisfy a girl in bed, and then he wants to screw around and dump her just because of his own issues. Holy fuck, I can't even believe I just thought that.

Ashley's still looking up at me. Lips parted. Shaking. Crying.

Don't cry, Princess. Fuck, she just closed her eyes. I could kiss her right now. I kind of want to kiss her right now.

I lean down. I'll do it. Fuck, this is stupid. Our lips are almost touching. She sees me. She opens her eyes. We're close. Way too close.

She pushes me away and looks around. "Do you have something I can blow my nose with?" she asks.

Mia Clark

# 5 - *Ashley*

DID HE ALMOST KISS ME? No way. Ugh. Weird?

Maybe I shouldn't have pushed him away. Wait, what am I saying? Did I want him to kiss me? Uh... no! I'm supposed to be smart, but I'm just acting like one of those bimbo girls Ethan likes to screw around with and then dump.

Why did I even tell him about what happened with Jake? I bet Ethan hasn't been in a real relationship in his entire life. What does he know? He probably agrees with Jake. It wouldn't surprise me.

He unwraps the towel from around his waist and hands it to me. "Here," he says.

I take it, staring at it, then I look at him. He's smiling at me, cocksure and confident. What an asshole.

"Um...?"

"You needed something to blow your nose with, right?" he says.

I laugh. "Ethan, this is a towel."

"Yeah, so?"

"I can't--"

He tries to take the towel to wipe my nose himself, but I pull it away from him. "Stop it," I snap. "Fine, alright?"

I blow my nose. Maybe this is a bad thing. I feel like I can smell him. Remember that melted sex thing I mentioned before? Yeah, that. It's like I'm rubbing the smell of his sexuality directly onto my nose, his pheromones making me crazy. Is that how that works? Is that why girls go wild over bad boy Ethan Colton? I kind of want to Google it. He'd probably call me a nerd if he knew.

Google, can bad boy pheromones make a girl go wild with lust?

"Let's get drunk," Ethan says. "It'll help you get over that stupid prick."

"Drunk?" I ask, laughing. I still have his towel up close to my face. I pinch it over my nose and blow. It's kind of gross and weird, but Ethan doesn't care. Why would he? He's the one who suggested it in the first place. Ugh, I can't believe I'm doing this.

"Yeah," he says. "Drunk. Watch a movie. Get some pizza. Whatever you want, your choice."

"We're eighteen," I remind him.

"Almost nineteen," he counters.

"Um, that's not twenty-one. How are we even going to get alcohol?"

"Mom and Dad are on vacation, remember, Princess?"

"Stop calling me that!"

"Yeah, whatever. Anyways, Little Miss Perfect, they're gone, and--"

He moves next to me, putting his hand on my waist to guide me towards where he wants me to look. I bristle and slap his hand, then I jump away. Ethan just laughs.

I see it, though. He points. Across the hall to the game room with a bar and liquor cabinet. Did I mention Ethan's father is rich? There's a full bar with a huge assortment of alcohol behind it, set into the wall in the game room, which is visible down the hall from the kitchen.

"There's probably some beer in the fridge, too," he adds, as if we needed more of an excuse to be irresponsible and do stupid things.

Ethan Colton never needs an excuse for either. It's what he's done since the day he was born.

I don't do things like this, though. I'm the good girl. I've always been the good girl.

Yes, and what did that get me? A stupid boyfriend who broke up with me because he couldn't go a couple of months without having sex.

Not even just sex with me, but sex with anyone, sex with someone else entirely. He's just like Ethan. Maybe worse. I can't believe I dated someone like that.

"You'll let me pick the pizza?" I ask. I'm angry. So angry that I'm considering Ethan's offer. Maybe it'll make me feel better.

"Yeah, whatever you want, Princess. Even that stupid ham and pineapple shit you like. If that's not the girliest pizza ever, I don't know what is."

"It's not girly," I say. "You're just... you're stupid, Ethan. That's what you are."

He laughs. "Great insult, Princess. Top of your game. I can see why everyone says you're smart."

"I hate you," I tell him, straight up. I'm not sure if I do hate him or not. I don't think I do. I actually really appreciate him trying to make me feel better. It's probably the nicest thing he's ever done. Probably the only nice thing he's ever done.

"Yeah, right back at you," he says, smirking. "But, hey, I'm going back in the pool. Want to join me? Then we can order food."

My mind wanders. Unfortunately. This is a bad thing. Joining Ethan in the pool? Just the two of us. Splashing, playing, wet, almost nothing between us but the thin cloth of our bathing suits. I have a bikini, even. His board shorts obviously don't hide all that much, going by the bulge I noticed from before. I mean, technically it's covered, but...

And we could be... in the pool... huh.

"N-no," I stammer. I need to stop thinking these things. I really do need to stop it.

"Suit yourself," he says. "If you change your mind you know where to find me."

He leaves and heads back outside to the pool. I watch him go, trying to convince myself this is a good idea. Or a bad idea. None of this is good.

I can't believe Mom left me here with him for the week. Alone. I can't believe I'm stuck with Ethan Colton alone for a week. I don't even want to know what kind of trouble he's going to get into. I refuse to be a part of it. I'm not like that.

Mia Clark

# 6 - *Ashley*

ONE NIGHT. That's it. I'll give in for just one night, and then tomorrow I'll go back to being regular. Because, I'm going to be completely honest here, I'm not sure that any of this is regular.

Ethan and I are watching a movie he's dubbed a chick flick. I guess I can't argue against that, but I think it has broader appeal, too. Yes, there's romance, but it's a romantic comedy, so it's funny. Everyone likes to laugh, right?

I get the feeling Ethan is laughing at me more than the movie, though. He keeps looking at me and grinning.

Probably because I'm drunk. No real way around that; yes, I'm drunk right now. More buzzed, I guess. I'm not falling over or being stupid, I'm just a bit tipsy and I'd like to eat more food.

"Pizza," I say, holding out my plate.

Ethan's taken it upon himself to be my personal servant for tonight. It's a nice change of pace. I deserve it, right? After what Jake did...

I don't want to think about that. I just want another slice of pizza.

"Here you go, Princess," Ethan says.

He gives me another slice of Hawaiian pizza, but not at all like I expected. He holds it out to me, up close to my mouth. Hey, why not? I'm drunk! Haha. It's funny, but maybe not. I'm one of those people, aren't I? I'm the silly drunk girl I told myself I'd never become. Um...

We've only had a couple of drinks, but it's fun to act like it's more. It's fun to be tipsy and give in and just relax and not worry about anything. I don't want to worry. I just want to have fun, and Ethan and I are having fun right now. It's fun for me, at least.

I open my mouth and he presses the pizza past my lips. I take a bite and start to chew. He puts the rest of my slice back on my plate.

"So, how's everything?" Ethan asks. "Feeling better?"

"You," I say, but then I forget the rest of what I was going to say. I chew and swallow, trying to remember. Oh! Right... "You're not supposed to be nice to me, Ethan Colton."

"You just had to add my last name in there, didn't you?" he says, grinning.

"Stop that grinning at me thing you're doing. I'm not going to fall for your good looks and charm."

I'm digging myself deeper here, aren't I? I'm going to blame it on the alcohol. It makes sense.

"Good looks and charm?" Ethan asks. And more grinning. Damn him!

If I'm blaming it on the alcohol, I really should get more. I should actually get fully drunk instead of just a bit tipsy. It makes sense in my head. "We should have more of those chocolate milk bombs," I say.

"You seriously just called it a chocolate milk bomb, didn't you?" he asks. "Way to ruin a good drink. Could you make it sound any more cute and innocent?"

"It is, though!" I say, shouting, laughing. I almost drop my pizza on the floor, but Ethan leans over and catches it. And me. He's holding me, keeping me steady. "It does taste like chocolate milk," I add. "I like it."

He's close now. Again. How close is he going to get to me. He's just helping me, I tell myself, remind myself. I'm a little buzzed right now. Partially inebriated. We had um... the chocolate milk bombs, and then some butterscotch schnapps shots. Just a quarter of a shot, so more like a sip, because I was scared. Ethan laughed at me about that one.

And this shot that tastes like a Snickers candy bar. Just a sip again, but I liked that one and I think

I could drink a whole shot. Oh! And Vodka. Ugh. Straight! Ethan laughed at me when I almost gagged on it. Somehow he drank it so smoothly. I don't know how he did it. I didn't even actually drink mine. I tasted it and then spit it out in the sink.

He's close now, though. Very close. I reach for my plate and my piece of pizza and lift it up, then hold it out for him. "Bite?" I ask.

He takes a bite, laughing at me. His arm is around me, hand on my hip, other hand close to my plate, making sure I don't drop it.

"I think you've had plenty to drink," he says. "Maybe we should take a break and just enjoy the movie."

"Your hand's on my hip," I tell him. Apparently I'm very subtle and smooth when I'm drunk, you don't even know. Ethan's had a lot more to drink than me. He's trying to play it off, but I can see him swaying a little, hesitating when he moves.

He shrugs and goes to move his hand away, to return to his own spot on the couch, but I stop him. I lean back and pin his hand behind me, keeping him from getting away from me.

My God, what am I doing? Not like I could pin Ethan in place if I wanted to. He plays football. I used to go to his games in high school. Not intentionally. I didn't go because of him. He was the quarterback, though. He was at the center of everything. It was hard not to notice Ethan play. *The* Ethan Colton.

He was good. He's still good. Even though his father could pay for his college education a hundred times over and then some, Ethan got a full football scholarship to a decent school. Not the best. It's still kind of a party school, I think, but I'm a little biased. Maybe. I don't know right now. Like I said before, I'm kind of tipsy.

Ethan's fingers grip my hip, pulling me back to reality. He's touching me. Again. But more. Holding me now. He leans close again. Too close. What's he doing?

"Hey, Princess, if you're going to keep my hand like that, you mind giving me another bite of pizza, at least?" he says with that sinfully sweet smile of his. It's a dangerous smile, and I know it. I don't know why I like looking at it so much then.

I offer him another bite of pizza. Then one for me. It takes me a second to parse through this, but... his lips... on the pizza... and then my lips...

Oh my God. There's a word for this but I can't remember. Secondhand kiss? Something. Um...

"Ethan, I'm drunk," I tell him. "You got me drunk."

He laughs at this, like I've just said the funniest thing in the world. It is kind of funny. I laugh, too.

"Never thought I'd see the day that the stuck up Little Princess got drunk," he says. Then, oddly, he adds, "Are you alright? Let's just take it easy with the drinks. I'm glad we could hang out like this, Ashley."

"Stop calling me Princess," I say. "I'm not stuck up, either! Just call me Ashley. It's not like you don't know my name."

"Yeah, who could forget? Ashley Banks, top of her class, always the goodie two-shoes. Every year. All the time. From second grade through high school, and now probably in college, too."

"Don't forget Kindergarten and first grade," I add.

"Hey, I didn't know you then. I was giving you a little slack. Maybe you weren't always a good girl."

"Well, I'm definitely not one now! We've been drinking! Ethan, I don't know if you know this, but this is illegal."

"It's only illegal if you get caught," he says, smirking. "We're just going to stay in tonight, Ashley. It's your night."

"My night." I say the words slowly. This is new and different. Jake never wanted to do what I wanted to do. I thought that's how relationships were. I thought it was the man's decision. Maybe because I'd never really been in one before. Not exactly, at least.

"What if I want to go wild, Ethan Colton? What then? What if I want to drive around the city and get into mischief?"

"Yeah, no," he says. "We've both been drinking, so that's not happening. I might be an asshole most of the time, but I'm not that stupid."

"Nuh uh," I say, sticking my tongue out at him. "You're pretty stupid."

"Wow, real mature, Princess."

"Why are you still holding me?" I ask him.

And, he is. Closer now. Intimate and nice. Just resting, his hand on my hip. He's closer than before. I offer him another bite of pizza, and he moves a little closer still.

"Just keeping my little sister safe," he says. "I'm the protective big brother."

"Shut up," I say. "We're the same age."

"I'm a month and ten days older than you," Ethan says, matter-of-fact. The way he says it makes me laugh.

"You're funny," I say. "That's good. Did you guess my birthday or what?"

"I know when your birthday is, Ashley. It's not that hard to remember."

I'd like to think that's it, but knowing Ethan I'm not really sure. I think there's something more to this. He's trying to trick me. I know it, I just don't know how. I'm too drunk to figure it out. That's not even true. I know I'm not actually drunk. Tipsy, yes, but it doesn't matter. I want to be irresponsible tonight. I don't want to worry about anything. I don't want to be the good girl right now.

I want to forget about everything that's happened to me today. It's easier if I blame it on the alcohol.

It's easy to forget some things, at least.

"You're sweet, Ethan," I tell him. "Sometimes you're sweet. Most of the time you're a jerk, though. I don't understand you at all."

"Oh, is that the game we're playing?" he asks. "You're smart, Ashley. Most of the time you're smart. Sometimes you're stupid, though. I don't understand you at all."

"Hey!" I said. "You... no, you can't do that. That's what I did."

"What's with this guy, Ashley? Jake, or whatever the hell his name is? Were you into him or what?"

"You called me stupid!" I say.

"You need to find somebody who's going to respect you," he says.

I feel like we're having entirely different conversations right now. I'm not sure what we're even talking about. I say something, but I don't even realize what I'm saying.

"Yeah, like you care. You don't respect anyone."

He stops. I stop. Everything gets cold between us, like we're two different people again. We're from two different worlds. Entirely different places. I don't know how I could ever think this was a good idea. I don't know why I thought it'd be nice to have a night of irresponsibility with Ethan. It wasn't. It's not.

"That's not true," he says, quiet. "I respect people."

"Oh yeah?" I ask. "Who?"

"You," he says, but he says it so fast that I think he's making it up, just saying something to say it, you know? After a couple of seconds, he adds, "Your mom, too. My dad."

"You sleep with girls," I say. "A lot of them. And then you just ditch them after. That's not a nice thing to do."

"Yeah, this was a mistake," he says. "I thought it'd be fun, but it's not."

He tries to get away again. Tries to pull his hand away from me.

"No," I say. "Stop. Ethan, wait. I'm sorry."

"Right, thanks," he says, but he's still pulling his hand away.

I drop my plate of pizza on the coffee table and grab his hand so he can't get away. I don't want it to be like this. I liked it before. I like laughing with Ethan and having fun and eating pizza, and...

Watching the movie. I look over. We can just watch the movie together, can't we? I hope he understands. What I see on the screen confuses me for a second, though. Um... they're kissing? Well, it is a romance movie, so I guess it makes sense.

It gives me an idea. I'm a little tipsy right now, which is what I"m going to use as an excuse for this stupid idea. Maybe Ethan is right. For a smart girl I sure can be stupid sometimes.

I throw myself onto him and I kiss him. The odd part is that after a second's hesitation, Ethan kisses me back. His hands are on me, around me, holding me, grabbing me. He pulls me closer to him. I'm on top of him, over him, close to him. My lips touch his and we kiss, frantic and fast. This is not at all like how Jake and I kissed. Not even remotely similar.

Oddly, this is very much like how I imagined it would be kissing Ethan.

This is getting heavy. Too heavy. His hands dig into the fabric of my pants, grabbing at my ass. I pull at his shirt, just pulling, not realizing that I'm kind of almost pulling like I want to pull it off, up and over his head. He stops, stops me, we stop.

"Ashley, we can't do this," he says.

"Wow, are you serious?" I ask. "You'll make out with any other girl, but not me? Am I not good enough for you?"

Where did that come from? I feel like maybe I'm projecting. Jake isn't Ethan, but Jake's an asshole, and I know Ethan's an asshole, so...

I cry. Sort of. It's not a lot, not like before. I'm feeling really emotional right now, though. Upset. I don't like it. I feel dizzy and angry and hurt and alone. My head hurts. I just want to... to kiss him. I just want him to hold me and tell me everything is going to be alright like he did before.

"Do you remember the first time we kissed?" I ask him. I don't know what brought this up, but it seems important right now.

"What?" he says. "What are you talking about?"

"You don't remember?" I ask again. "I guess it wasn't that memorable to you."

"Ashley, yes, I remember, alright? Are you happy now?"

Mia Clark

# 7 - Ethan

THIS ISN'T THE FIRST TIME I've kissed her, but I thought the last time was going to actually be the last.

We were young and impressionable or something like that. I didn't even think she'd remember it. I remember it, because... yeah, when you kiss someone like Ashley Banks, it's real fucking hard to forget.

It happened about six months after our parents got married. She and her mom moved into our place. Didn't really expect that. I was kind of used to being alone. Dad was always working, so I got the run of the place. He had some tutor for me that I kind of just ignored most of the time, and she left as soon as Dad got home, anyways.

My dad and her mom went away for the weekend once, though. I convinced him we were old enough to stay home by ourselves. I mean, fuck, we were fifteen, almost sixteen, which should have been fine, right? Yeah, it would have been, except I had an ulterior motive.

Party time! Aw yeah!

I swear Little Miss Perfect Princess Ashley nearly died. I thought she was going to call her mom and tell her everything, too, but for whatever reason she didn't. Who knows why? Maybe she had potential. Party girl potential? Yeah, something like that.

I invited a bunch of kids from school over, ordered a million boxes of pizza. Had to get it from a bunch of different places, because for whatever reason they thought I was kidding when I said I wanted twenty pizzas. Do you even know who I am? My dad's a billionaire. I can afford twenty pizzas.

Whatever. Fuck them.

Anyways, everything's going well. We've got soda, pizza, more candy than Willy Wonka, and an entire fucking mansion to ourselves. Which is probably a really bad thing to give to a reckless group of high school kids, but whatever. That was kind of the entire point.

Shit happened. A lot of it. It ended up devolving into games of Truth or Dare, which mostly seemed like an excuse for people to dare each other to make out in a closet. Which, I might have done at least once. Ashley was there, of course. Standing off to the side. Yeah, right, didn't think Miss Perfect Princess would join in on that one. Obviously.

She took the whole thing well. Well enough. It was a weekend, but everyone went home by nine, and we sort of started cleaning up a little, but she was pissy and prissy and acting like a goddamn princess again.

"What's your issue?" I remember asking her.

"Nothing!" she screamed.

"This is like that PMS shit, isn't it?" I asked.

"You're an idiot, Ethan Colton!"

"I thought chocolate helped that. We've got plenty. Go stuff your face with it."

"Loser."

Remembering the way she said that makes me laugh, even to this day.

"Look, what's wrong?" I asked. "Did you have fun tonight or what?"

There was something. I didn't know what. I still don't know what it was. It's hard to tell with her. Ashley is confusing as fuck. Don't even get me started on that. If I had to put a word to the look in her eyes, though, I'd say it was a twinkle. Some sort of spark. Shit. I don't know.

"No," she said. "I didn't."

"What the fuck, why not?" Yeah, I had a mouth, even then. What of it?

"I wanted to play, too," she said. "I wanted to kiss someone."

I forget if I was feeling vindictive or honest, but I said, "No one would have kissed you anyways."

She almost cried. Fuck, she was going to cry, wasn't she? I didn't mean it in a bad way, but it was true. No one would have. Not with me here. Yeah, she was my stepsister, but it was practically the same thing as being my sister, right? Or something like that. No one wanted me to kick their ass, and I think I very well might have.

Ashley was nice. She wasn't that kind of girl. She didn't fuck around, not with anything. She was the kind of girl that went far in life. Not like me. What was I? Some brat. Spoiled rich kid who screwed around and relied on the fact that his father had plenty of money to keep him set for life. Which was true. No shame in admitting it. I'm not going to lie about it or anything.

Anyways, she was crying, and I don't know what the fuck I was thinking, but...

"Truth or dare?" I asked her.

"Everyone's left already," she said, sniffling. "It's not the same."

"Look, you're the one crying about it, so truth or dare, Ashley?"

She gave me the most ornery, obstinate, stubborn, determined look I've ever seen on anyone. "Dare," she said. "I dare someone to kiss me! There! Are you happy--"

Well, fuck, no, I wasn't happy. What fun was a dare if there was no one to do it? So I did it. Well, fuck me, yeah, not one of my brightest moves in the world, but she was over here crying about it, so what the hell?

It was kind of awkward. At first, at least. She looked completely shocked when my lips touched hers, but I kept going. And tongue. Yeah, I'm good at this shit, don't you forget it. Even at fifteen I was strong, too. Had been playing football since middle school, lifting weights for a couple years now.

I put my hands on her hips, held her close, and kissed her like anyone should be happy to kiss her. She still had glasses then, and I'd never kissed a girl with glasses before, so our noses kind of bumped together and tilted her frames to the side. She pulled her glasses off and dropped them onto the dining room table nearby, then cupped my cheeks in her hands and kissed me again.

Shit, that was good. Real good. Great memories.

I think we might have gone further if we had the chance. Maybe a lot further. I'd known this girl for most of my life, and now she was living under the same roof as me. How fucked would that be?

Good thing our parents came home. Maybe it was good. I mean, it wasn't that good. I got grounded for that one. For a long time. They weren't even supposed to be home yet. We were supposed to have another day on our own. It was probably good we didn't. I could have kissed Ashley Banks for hours. Shit, she was good.

Alas, it was not meant to be. I just remember my dad screaming from the front door, presumably after seeing the trash we'd left laying around everywhere.

"Ethan Albert Colton!"

We froze. The both of us. The last thing that happened was Ashley staring into my eyes. Maybe. Girl was blind as a bat without her glasses, so who the fuck knows what she was looking at?

"Albert?" she asked.

I rolled my eyes at her and pushed her away. "Go hide in your room and pretend you're asleep. I'll take the blame for everything."

# 8 - *Ashley*

THAT WAS MY FIRST KISS," I tell him. "You were my first."

"Shit," Ethan says. "No fucking way? Are you serious?"

"Yes. No one else would kiss me."

"I don't know why not," he says.

"What's that supposed to mean?" I ask. It certainly can't mean what I think it means.

"It means," Ethan says, his voice a little hesitant, but still genuine, "that if our parents hadn't come home and interrupted us, I would have gladly spent the rest of the weekend kissing you."

No. I shake my head. That can't be true. "Liar," I say.

"Don't fucking tempt me, Ashley," he says with a growl. "Just don't fucking tempt me. You don't know what you're dealing with here."

"You can't do anything," I say. "You won't. Everyone might think you're a bad boy, Ethan, but I know you. You're not as bad as they think."

"Just keep it up, Princess. I dare you."

I don't know if he meant it that way, but it brings back memories. Good ones.

"Truth or dare?" I ask.

"Yeah, sure, go for it," he says with a wicked grin.

"If I dare you, you have to do it," I remind him. "No matter what. What happens if you don't?"

"You think I won't?"

I shake my head, no. "Nope!"

"Alright, if I don't do it, I'll quit the football team," he says.

"You can't quit the football team!" I shout, then I laugh when I realize how loud I'm being over something so silly. "Ethan, you can't quit. That's what your scholarship is for. If you quit you won't have money for college."

"I'm not going to quit, because whatever you dare me to do, I'm sure as hell going to do it."

"I really doubt it. I can think of a lot of dares you won't do."

"Oh yeah?" he says. And then it comes. He forces me into it. "I dare you to dare me, Ashley. If you don't, you need to wait on me hand and foot for the entire week that Mom and Dad are gone."

I open my mouth to say something, to protest. I should especially protest because I never agreed to that. I don't know if I would ever agree to that. This isn't a pre-planned thing, you know? It's just kind of spur of the moment. That's what makes it fun, though. I feel free. I feel relaxed and nice and Ethan and I were just kissing, and I really did like that. I loved our first kiss before, too. My first kiss ever. I knew he'd kissed other girls before. I definitely knew he'd kissed other girls after. And I knew that he...

"Fuck me, Ethan Colton," I say, throwing caution to the wind; mostly because I know he won't. "Bring me upstairs and fuck me. I dare you. I know you won't."

"Oh, don't be so fucking sure of yourself, Princess."

Mia Clark

# 9 - Ashley

'M IN ETHAN'S BED. Naked. We're both naked. He's on top of me, his cock is inside me. Oh my God. I can't even begin to describe how this feels. It's unlike anything I've ever felt before.

Ethan is unlike anyone I've ever been with. Which probably isn't saying a lot. I've only had sex with a few people before, and it was all... *not very good.*

I just thought it was me. I believed Jake when he said that I wasn't very good, except Ethan certainly seems to be enjoying himself.

I laugh and kiss him and he thrusts hard into me, burying his cock deep inside of me. His lips wrap around my throat, sucking hard.

"Something funny, Princess?" he asks.

I wrap my arms around his back and dig my nails into his skin, raking them down, leaving thin red scratch lines. I like how Ethan doesn't even stop, doesn't even care.

"You feel so good inside me," I whisper into his ear, purring, seductive.

"Damn fucking straight," he says. "God, you're like a fucking vice around my cock."

"Do you like it?" I ask him.

"Yeah," he says.

"Why did you stop, then?"

"Give me a fucking break, you insatiable freak."

He pulls out of me, then rams back in. Hard. I can feel it, can feel him. His bed bounces beneath the force of our bodies becoming one. Ethan grabs one of my breasts, squashing it in his hand. He pulls back, then buries his mouth against my nipple, sucking hard, nibbling. I arch my back up, but he pushes me back down, shoving me onto the bed. Letting go of my breast, he grabs my hips, then slams in, out, in out, fast, pistoning hard into me.

"Fuck, you're tight, Princess," he says.

"Stop," I say. "Ashley. Call me Ashley."

"I'll call you whatever I damn well please," he says.

"Ethan," I murmur. "I... I think I'm... I've never..."

"You about to cum?" he asks. "You've never had an orgasm before?"

"Not with anyone else."

"Well, shit, I better play my A game. I didn't realize."

Holy fuck. This isn't his best? It's really good. Ethan does more, though. Oh God.

His hips grind against mine, his pelvis rubbing against my pubis. My clit. I can feel it, feel the tensing muscles of his abs as he thrusts hard into me, then presses against my sensitive pearl. I didn't know this was possible. I didn't know this was a thing someone could do, but here Ethan is, doing it.

I'm a little lightheaded from the drinks, and certainly not thinking straight--that's what I want to tell myself, because why else would I be doing this?--but that doesn't stop me from spasming in a writhing, hot mess on the bed as soon as my orgasm hits me. I shake. I literally shake! I'm trembling and my legs are quivering and my mouth keeps opening and closing on its own. Ethan laughs and he kisses me hard, shoving his tongue in my mouth. It's so rough but amazing. I didn't know something like this would feel so good.

I kiss him. Oh, I kiss him. It reminds me of the first time we kissed. When we were interrupted. I thought he hated me, thought he just did it to favor me, but then his father shouted at him. He took all the blame... *for me?* He got in a lot of trouble for that.

I still don't know if he likes me, but right now Ethan Colton is on top of me, fucking me hard, laughing, rampant, as my body writhes and wriggles beneath him in orgasm.

"Fuck, Ashley," he says. "That's goddamn delicious. I love the look on your face. You're beautiful."

I don't even know how, but Ethan stays true to his word, to the dare. He doesn't stop until I'm too tired to move, which has to be hours later. I don't even remember stopping, but the next thing I know I'm in a kind of hazy afterglow of intoxicating pleasure and he's curled up next to me, near me, cuddling with me. We're under the blankets.

"I'm tired, Ethan," I whine. "Can you get me a glass of water?"

He shifts and sidles away from me, then goes to his private bathroom and brings me a glass of tap water. "Here," he says, offering it to me. He holds it close to my lips and tilts it so I can drink without sitting up.

I swallow the cool liquid, savoring it. Sex is a lot of work. Or drinking water is. One of those. We just had sex, didn't we? Yessss... I'm not sure how this happened. I kind of feel like this is a bad thing, but I'm too tired to worry about it now. I'm not sure if I'm even tipsy anymore, I'm just tired now.

"Hey, go to sleep," Ethan says.

I close my eyes and do just that.

# 10 - Ethan

Y EAH, WELL, FUCK.

Not sure what else to say besides that. Just fuck. That one word seems to sum up everything that happened pretty well, anyways. No reason to get all poetic and creative over it, now is there?

The problem with all of this is that, uh... how do I put this without sounding like an asshole?

Eh, fuck it, I'm already an asshole. Why stop now?

I'm just going to be straight with you: Ashley's pussy is fucking delicious.

Not in the literal sense, though I really wouldn't mind finding out sometime, but that was possibly the best sex I've ever had. Not even *possibly.* It is. Hands down, the best. She's so goddamn *responsive.* It's like everything I did turned her on. It's not even *like* it did, I'm *positive* it did. I can't even understand why her ex-boyfriend would break up with her just because he needed to go two months without sex. I've known this girl for over ten years now and I almost feel like I'd gladly wait another decade just for round two.

Another decade? Shit, she's sleeping in bed right next to me.

I really can't understand this, though. Is this really Ashley? For some reason, it's not that hard to believe. I do kind of feel like a dick, though. We probably shouldn't have done that. I probably should have stopped it before it started.

I probably should have done a lot of things, but I can't even make myself regret having some of the best sex of my life with this girl.

She said she's never had an orgasm during sex before? Fuck, she could have fooled me. She's good. This girl is good. I do not even know what to say about how good she is.

Delicious as fuck, that's what she is.

I'm tired, though. She wore me out. Let me sleep on this and let you know how I feel in the morning.

# 11 - Ashley

WAKE UP AND I'M SORE. A good sore, though. A pleasant, tingling ache, and with the blankets surrounding me like a warm cloud, I feel nice. I have my head on a pillow and my leg wrapped around a leg, my arm on a chest, and...

Wait, um... my leg... and arm...?

I open my eyes to figure out what's going on, because Jake never lets me sleep with him in his dorm room and he never stays in mine, either. It kind of bothers me, because I know plenty of girls who stay over with their boyfriends sometimes, or boys who stay with their girlfriends. It's not exactly allowed as per dorm rules, but everyone does it anyways.

I'm sure Jake won't let me stay over because he knows me. Right...? He doesn't want me breaking the rules, since even in college I've built up a reputation for being the good girl rule follower. I just... it's not like that's a big rule, you know? It's not like it's actually important. We won't get in that much trouble. We'll just get talked to about it, at most, and otherwise it's no big deal.

I can't think about this right now, though. I have a headache, too. I feel weird. What happened last night?

I shift my leg a little and feel skin against skin, mine soft and supple against tight, muscular legs. Speaking of muscle, the chest my arm is draped over is nice, too. Strange? Has Jake been working out?

I sneak over to offer him a good morning kiss, and that's when I realize exactly what happened.

This isn't Jake. Ethan's laying there, staring at me, smiling. I almost kissed him! On the lips! Ew. Gross, disgusting, that's...

Holy shit! We slept together. Not just sleeping, but literally we... we had sex. Together. In his bed. In our mom and dad's house. In...

This is a problem. A big problem. Big big big problem. I scramble away from him and nearly roll off my side of the bed in the process. I probably should just do that, I probably should get out of bed, run away, go back to my room, but then I realize I'm naked. And, judging by what I felt before, Ethan is naked, too.

"Hey, good morning, Princess," he says, nonchalant.

"What the fuck?" I say. I try not to swear, I really do, but this is Ethan, and we're at home, and I feel like this is definitely a "what the fuck?" type of moment, don't you?

"Nice to see you, too," he says, flashing me a devilish grin. Yes, that's right. Devilish. Demonic. What the heck was he thinking?

Then I remember it was my idea. Yes, we were both drinking. I'm not sure either of us should have been coming up with ideas, to be honest, but this one was definitely mine. A dare. I didn't think he'd do it. I didn't want him to quit the football team, but he's always just so cocksure and confident and I wanted to knock him down a peg or two.

I think. I think that's what I was thinking. Now I'm not so sure, because along with the memories of why I dared him to do what he did comes the memories of what exactly it felt like for him to do it.

He was so *hard*. I mean, yes, that's how sex works, Ashley. I remind myself this, and it almost makes me laugh, but it's not funny. It's not! But Ethan was different. He was so vibrant and alive, his erection pulsing and pressing inside me. It felt so good. And he knew exactly what to do, too. I felt like I knew exactly what to do when I was with him. Or was that the alcohol? Did it lower our inhibitions and... well, of course it lowered our inhibitions. I mean, I just woke up in bed with my brother.

Stepbrother, I remind myself. As if that's any better! Yes, he's been my stepbrother for about three years now, but I've known him since second grade, so...

Shit. Shit shit shit. Shit. I can't believe we did this. This was a huge mistake. It's still a mistake. I tell him as much.

"I need to go. Please, Ethan, look away. Where are my clothes? I need to get dressed. I need to go."

"What's the hurry?" he asks, as if he hasn't realized what the issue is. Is it just my issue then? I feel like he should have an issue, too.

"Ethan, this was a huge mistake. I was drunk. You were drunk. I was vulnerable."

I'm making excuses now, and I know it. Yes, I still think this was a mistake, but I liked what happened, too. Not um... not the sex. No, I did like that, too. On a physical level, at least. Wow. Orgasms during sex are nice. I belatedly realize exactly what I was just thinking right there. Orgasms... plural. Yup. No real way around that. I had more than one, and they were all good.

I just... no, we shouldn't have had sex, but I liked the closeness. The playfulness. I liked eating pizza with him, watching a movie. I even liked drinking and being irresponsible, but...

This is bad. Very bad. He's rubbing off on me. Resident bad boy Ethan Colton is turning me into an irresponsible bad girl. I can just imagine him calling me his naughty girl and... and what? Spanking me?

STOP! Stop it, Ashley! Cut it out! I have to yell at myself to bring this all to a halt or I'm not sure what's going to happen next.

"Yeah, sorry," Ethan says.

This surprises me. Ethan's saying sorry? When has that ever happened before. "What?" I ask.

"Look, I didn't mean for that to happen. I don't want you to get the wrong idea here. I never thought things would go that far."

"Well, good," I say. "Now can you please go away so I can get dressed and we can forget all about this? Maybe it never happened. Maybe we were just so drunk that we think it did and all we did was fall asleep."

Ethan laughs, but we both know what I said isn't true. "Yeah, maybe," he says. "Look, I'll go make breakfast or something. You hang out here, take your time, whatever. How's your head?"

"It hurts a little," I admit. "I'm thirsty, too. I don't... I don't feel good."

And it's so weird to say these things, because this is Ethan. He's naked. In bed. We were naked in bed together. We had sex. I can't even begin to get over this. What the heck! Yes, good. Heck. That's better. I'm reverting back to my previous self. I'm not like this. I'm not some sex-crazed rulebreaker.

But I do like Ethan. Sort of. He's not so bad sometimes. He's even nice sometimes, too. In an arrogant asshole sort of way. He wanted to make me feel better last night with pizza and drinking and a movie. I never would have expected that. I would have expected him to just go out partying with some friends while leaving me home alone to wallow in self pity.

Not that what he did was much better in the end, though. Leaving me to wallow in self pity or having sex with me? Which was the better option?

I can't even believe this happened.

Ethan gets out of bed and he's definitely absolutely completely naked. I can see his butt. Ethan Colton, my stepbrother, is naked in front of me, his sexy, tight ass bared for me and me alone, and when he steps over to find his pants, I see more than a glimpse of his cock. It should be soft. Right? Um... no...

What's that thing with men? They wake up with erections sometimes, right? I don't know. I've never really thought about this before, but, yes, Ethan is definitely erect. Somewhat erect. I don't think he's as erect as he was last night when he was on top of me, thrusting into me, when I was climaxing around his cock, right before he...

Oh my God, Ethan came inside me. Oh my God. I can't even...

"What?" he asks, looking at me. "What's with the look?"

"You came inside me," I say. "You didn't wear a condom."

"Shit!" he says. "Wait, you're on birth control, right? I thought you were."

"Well, yes, I am. Wait a second... how would you know?"

He shrugs, nothing doing. "Sometimes your mom would ask me to pick some stuff up, and I'd get your prescriptions, too."

"What the hell? My mom sent you to get my birth control?"

"It's not that big a deal, Princess."

"Stop," I say. "Ethan, stop it. Please, just stop. Don't call me that. I'm Ashley. I'm your sister. I don't like what's going on here."

"Yeah, well, I'm gone. Do whatever you want. I'll be downstairs making breakfast if you want something."

"I don't think I do," I say. "I don't think I can talk to you right now."

Mia Clark

# 12 - Ashley

ETHAN LEFT ONCE HE PUT HIS PANTS ON, but he magically forgot his shirt. Magically? I think he's doing this on purpose. I don't know why. I really don't understand him. Why's he walking around shirtless? Granted, he was shirtless yesterday, too, but that was when he'd just come inside from the pool, so it made sense. Sort of, at least.

And just because I'm on birth control makes it fine for him to cum inside me? Um... no! Weird. Gross. Ugh. I've never done that before. I kind of liked it. At the time. Not now. Now it's disturbing. Disgusting.

I can't help remembering it, though. I didn't even realize it at the time, but then he bent down to whisper into my ear. "I'm about to, Ashley," he said. "I'm gonna cum."

And... I think he was going to pull out? I think? I'm not sure now. It felt like it, but maybe he was just pulling back to thrust back into me. Deep. He was definitely deep. I pulled him back. Sort of. I had my arms wrapped around him and when he started to pull out of me I clung tight to his torso and pulled him back close to me. And then...

I can't think about this anymore. Ew. Ugh. What's wrong with me? I'm not supposed to like that.

Ethan Colton is my stepbrother and he's also the only man to ever give me an orgasm during sex, and he's also incredible in bed. There, I said it. I admitted it. It's over now, right? Acceptance is the first step to... what? This isn't that. It's not that at all!

I'm going to go to my room and sleep and stay there and wait until my mom and his dad come back from their vacation. Maybe I'll call her. What the heck, what am I going to say to her? Mom, I just had sex with Ethan, and it was a huge mistake, but I kind of liked it. I liked it at the time, I mean. I don't like it now.

I can smell him cooking breakfast. I hate him. Why is he doing this to me? It smells so good. I roll and cuddle with Ethan's blankets, taking in the scent of him, his masculine warmth, along with the savory smell of eggs, cooked onions, mushrooms, sausage, and... he's making pancakes. That asshole is making pancakes. I love pancakes. With maple syrup. Mmm... and his father always gets the best kind, too. Fresh and thick, and...

Fine. You know what? I'm going to go have breakfast. I don't care.

I throw off the blankets and jump out of bed. Yes, I'm naked, but it doesn't matter because I'm alone. I tiptoe around Ethan's room looking for my clothes. Why is my bra under his dresser? How did that even happen? I stoop to pick it up and put it back on fast. For whatever reason, my panties are hanging out of his bedside table's drawer, too. I snatch them up and slip them on, and then, because I'm here and I'm curious, I open the drawer and look inside.

Right there. Right there! Right on top and right there, as plain as day, is a box of condoms. The asshole could have worn a condom at least, but, no, he didn't. I can't believe this. I slam the drawer shut and go to find my pants, which are under his bed. I don't even know where my shirt is, but then I see it hanging over a lamp.

Oh my God, what did we do in here? This is crazy.

I'm not going to think about it anymore, though. No, I refuse. It's not my fault, it's his. It was his idea to get drunk. And he was the one who accepted my dare. He seduced me. He's the one who thrust his thick, throbbing cock deep inside me. He's the one who didn't wear a condom. He's the one who came inside me. He's...

He's the one who went downstairs to make me breakfast.

What a prick.

# 13 - Ethan

WAS JUST GOING TO MAKE AN OMELET and a side of sausage, but then I remember that Ashley loves pancakes. I like them, too. My dad gets this amazing maple syrup. We used to have pancakes every Sunday as a treat after...

After my mom died. That was before, when Dad actually stayed home for the weekend. Then he got bogged down from work, or so he said. I was alone more often than not after that. I guess it wasn't alone, considering I always had someone here with me, but that's not the same. It's not the same as spending time with your dad on the weekend making pancakes.

I mix up a batch real quick and add it to the list of things to cook. Shouldn't take long. The stove has enough burners for everything, so it'll be quick, regardless.

Why the fuck am I making pancakes? Shit, this confuses the fuck out of me. Can't really deny that pancakes are great, though. Who cares if Ashley loves them? I sure don't. That's not why I'm doing this. That's what I tell myself, anyways.

While I'm fixing everything up, I get into a zone. I should record this. Send it in as an audition tape for Hell's Kitchen or something. Who the fuck is Gordon Ramsay? I'm Ethan Colton, bitch! America's Next Top Chef.

Nah, sounds like a lot of work. Also, I doubt chefs get a lot of action, if you know what I mean. Yeah, cooking is cool and all, but it's not exactly a pussy magnet. Unless you make pancakes for a girl who loves them, I guess.

Shit, I'm done. What the hell am I doing? I can't even begin to understand myself. This is seriously fucked up.

While I'm out of it and cooking, Ashley comes down. She's wearing the same clothes from last night, which only stands to remind me of when I ripped them off of her, revealing her soft, begging body.

Shit.

I remember kissing her. Not just her kissable lips, but her neck. I remember whispering into her ear, asking her if she really wanted to do this. You can take it back, Ashley. You don't have to dare me.

No, she said. I'm not letting you out of it that easily, Ethan Colton.

Alright, Princess. Don't have to tell me twice.

I should have stopped anyways. I really should have. But, you know what? Fuck. Burying my cock into her tight, slick pussy was like waking up from a goddamn dream. I never knew what I was missing before that, but now that I do...

Shit.

"I'm joining you for breakfast," she says, huffy and prissy, sitting on a stool at the breakfast bar. "Please make some for me, too."

# 14 - Ashley

THAN SMIRKS AT ME, giving me a sidelong glance while he prepares food. "Yeah, already done. I knew you'd come down."

I hate him. I just hate him. I can't believe how arrogant and cocky he is. He knew I'd come down? How? How did he know? He didn't. He's just acting like he did. And it frustrates me! It makes me mad. It's not nice. It's rude and arrogant and frustrating.

"Stop acting like you know me, Ethan," I tell him. "Because, you don't. What happened last night was a mistake and I'm going to forget about it."

"That bad, huh?" he asks, flipping one of the pancakes, then going to turn over the omelet he's working on.

I don't know how to answer him. Should I lie? Yes, it was bad. Horrible. No, that's only going to bother me more later. I don't lie. I'll just... I'll...

"Listen," I say. "Ethan, as reluctant as I am to admit it, I enjoyed what happened, but it wouldn't have happened if I wasn't drunk."

"You trying to say it was only good because you were drunk?" he asks. "We were both drinking, Princess. We didn't even have that much."

"Probably," I say, though I don't know if that's true or not. If I believe it enough, I think it can be true, though.

Ethan has the audacity to laugh. He tosses both the pancakes from the pan into a plate, then pours enough batter for two more into the hot pan. Gliding to the fridge, he opens the door and pulls out the maple syrup, reaches for a fork and a knife from the drawer nearby, too, and then slips over to bring it all to me. Two pancakes on a plate, a fork and knife, and maple syrup. I'm the first to eat.

"It's not funny," I say. "It's really not, Ethan."

"Look, Princess, I don't mean to be the one to tell you this, but it would have been just as good if we weren't buzzed. Probably better."

Better? My mind begins to consider the possibilities, and... I don't know if I like this. I decide to ignore him and focus on the food in front of me instead. I take a bite, chew, savoring the soft fluffiness of the pancake mixed with the thick sweetness of the syrup. Oh my God, these are good. Ethan's a good cook. A year after me and my mom moved in with him and his dad, we were all at dinner once and his dad mentioned how he and Ethan used to have pancakes every weekend after my mom brought up how much I loved them.

And... well, one thing led to another, which led to us having pancakes every Saturday for awhile after that. Until we both went to college. It's almost the same now, but without our parents. Oh, and the fact that we woke up in bed naked with each other. That's definitely not the same as then.

He's staring at me. One of the omelets is finished, and he's putting a handful of sausages on a plate with it, flipping pancakes, another omelet...

I need to stop this. I need to.

"We won't ever know now," I say. "It's done. It was a mistake."

"Yeah," Ethan says. "Too bad."

I splutter and nearly choke on my pancake. Ethan smirks at me, some mischievous bad boy grin on his face. Why is he doing that? Why does he do it? It's so... it's attractive, but he's not supposed to be attractive to me! Stop it!

He gets a glass from one of the cabinets above the sink, then a carton of orange juice from the fridge, fills the glass, and brings it to me.

"Don't choke, Princess," he says.

I drink some of the juice, washing down my pancake along with my regret, then I glare at him.

"Why?" I ask him. "Just tell me why? Why are you making fun of me? It was a mistake, alright? I shouldn't have done that. You shouldn't have, either. Neither of us should have. But that's not the point. You don't have to make fun of me about it, too."

"Huh?" he says, lifting one brow, looking at me like I'm the crazy one.

"Too bad?" I say. "What's that supposed to mean?"

"It means what it means," he says. "Too bad we won't find out. Like you said, too bad we won't ever know."

"Oh, and you want to know? You aren't at all bothered by the fact that we had sex? Your dad is married to my mom, you know?"

"Look, I get it," he says, but I don't think he does. "It's weird. I didn't want it to happen, either, but it did. It's not like we're actually related, though."

While he's telling me this, he finishes up with the rest of the food. He brings me my omelet and sausage, then puts his, along with his pancakes, opposite me at the breakfast bar. After pouring himself a glass of orange juice, he joins me.

"Ethan, it doesn't matter. We can't do it again," I say.

"Why not?" he asks.

It's a weird question. It's not a request, or him begging me to reconsider, it's more of an act of rebellion. He's just trying to tease me, to ruffle my feathers, to...

I don't know what he's trying to do, but I don't like it.

"I think..." I pause to figure out how to word this. "I think I was just feeling vulnerable last night, Ethan. Alright? I know you might not understand that, because you don't have serious relationships,

but I was dating Jake for a few months and then after everything that happened, it was just hard."

He shrugs and nods. "Alright, but what's that have to do with us?"

"What do you mean what's it have to do with us? I think it's kind of obvious, don't you?"

"I get it, Princess," he says; but when I scowl at him he changes his mind. "Ashley, I get it. It happens. Rebound relationships, right? Whatever you want to call it. Happens to the best of us."

I roll my eyes at him, because obviously it doesn't; it doesn't happen to him.

"Maybe you were feeling vulnerable," he says. "I can understand that. Your douchebag boyfriend told you that he wanted to break up with you so he could have sex with other woman over the summer. It makes sense for you to get pissed about that. And, yeah, maybe because of that you were thinking that you aren't good enough in bed or something? Fuck if I know."

It's annoying, because he's kind of right. Yes, that's what I was thinking. What's his point?

"For what it's worth, I think you're good," Ethan says. "And, yeah, fuck it, that might be a little weird to say, but you know me, always causing trouble, so there you go."

"Thanks, I think," I say. I'm still not sure where he's going with this. "What's this have to do with what you said before?"

"Mom and Dad are gone for the week. We've already had sex. Yeah, it was a mistake, and yeah, it's kind of awkward now--"

"Kind of?" I ask. "Um, it's very awkward, Ethan."

He smirks and takes a big bite of his pancake. "Yeah, it is, huh?"

Finally! Finally he admits it. Thank God!

"It really is," I say.

"I get it," he says. "But it's done. It happened. Maybe it'll help. Rebound relationships suck. I've seen it all before. I've been a part of it. You might have an opinion of me, and I can't say it's wrong, but I don't want to be that dick that makes a girl feel like shit, Ashley. I just want us both to have a good time."

I narrow my eyes at him, because this sounds like he's trying to say something without actually saying it, but... no, then he says it.

"If that's what you need, I'm here for you. Rebound or whatever. We can go into it without any expectations, just get it out of your system, make you feel better, and then you can move on to a boyfriend who's not a fucking asshole like whatever the fuck his name was that dumped you over some stupid shit."

"Wait. Stop. Hold on. Let me see if I'm following you," I say; he nods, waiting for me to continue. "We had sex, and it was a mistake, and so now you're saying that we can do it again, as a rebound relationship thing, to get it out of my system, boost my confidence or something, and then just stop, act like it's all over, and I'll date someone else?"

Because, really, that sounds like the stupidest thing I've ever heard, but I'm pretty sure that's what he's suggesting right now.

"Yeah, kind of," he says. "Like friends with benefits. Just go into it with clear expectations so no one gets hurt, and then be done with it, easy as that."

"That's not easy," I say.

"We've already had sex, Princess. It's not hard. It's the exact same thing, just with less alcohol."

"Ethan, we're not exactly friends. You're my stepbrother."

He shrugs. "Friends with benefits, stepbrother with benefits, what the fuck's the difference?"

"First off, when you swear like that it makes you sound like an idiot."

He laughs and chomps down on a sausage.

"Second, it's not that easy still."

"A week," he says. "Mom and Dad are gone for a week. No one has to know. I won't tell anyone. Promise. You can say a lot about me, but I'm not the kiss and tell type."

"What!" I practically shout. Because, no, that can't be true. But he just smirks at me.

And... the more I think about it, the more it does seem to be true. Yes, I know Ethan's um... seduced? He's slept with a lot of girls, but he never really talks about it. They seem to talk about it, though. I remember hearing girls gossiping about it in high school, having to listen to them talk about him and how he brought them somewhere fancy and nice, how his dad is rich and...

It was really awkward when my mom married his dad and I kept having to hear these same things, and even see these girls come over sometimes, seeing Ethan leave with one of them, or...

That night, the party. Nothing too much happened, but I saw him making out with Stacy Alcott.

And then later he was kissing me.

"It's your choice," Ethan says. He's finished with his food already, somehow, and he takes his plates and tosses them in the sink. "Here, tell you what, I'm going upstairs to take a shower. I'll give you until I'm done to make up your mind. Come up and tell me if you want to go through with it. Just a week, just while your mom and my dad are on vacation. No one will ever know, and after that we can go back to normal."

I glare at him, because I'm not sure if he's being serious or not.

"If you come up, I'll take it as a yes. We live in the same house. You know where to find me," he says, winking.

The way he says it is funny. Kind of funny. I don't want to laugh, but I accidentally crack a smile, and Ethan smiles back at me. What's that look in his eyes? It's not a good look, at any rate; definitely a dangerous look.

"If I finish my shower and I don't see you, then that's a no," he says. "I won't bother you about it, Princess. You do you, make up your own mind. I'm here to help if you want, that's all."

That's all? *That's all?* Is he being serious? I think he is, but I don't know for sure, and I can't ask him now. I don't think I could ever ask him. He doesn't say anything else, doesn't wait for me to speak. No, he just leaves. He walks out of the kitchen and heads down the hall to the stairs, presumably to go to his bedroom and then shower.

He has his own bathroom, just like I do, private and connected to his bedroom. If I want to answer him, if I decide to agree to his stupid plan, I have to walk through his bedroom, step past his bed, and go into his bathroom. All the while with memories of what happened between us last night fogging up my mind, being able to see the bed we were in, being able to remember the creak and groan of the box spring, of the headboard smacking against the wall, of...

Why am I even thinking about this? Obviously I'm not going to agree to his stupid plan. I'm just going to sit here, finish up my omelet and pancakes, then my sausage, and when he finishes showering, I'll just go take a shower of my own. In my own bathroom. With my door locked, just in case. So he doesn't get any ideas, you know?

I chew. And swallow. Hard. Again. Ethan really does make good pancakes. I hate him. I hate that he makes good pancakes. I hate that he's good at sex. Who even says that? Good at sex? I hate that he's the first person I've been with that's given me an orgasm during sex. This wouldn't be the same otherwise. If he'd just not given me an orgasm, or if I'd had orgasms during sex before, then...

What? I don't know.

Something kind of hits me around this time, though. Why haven't I had an orgasm during sex before? Was it the alcohol? No, unlikely. Yes, I don't know exactly, because, no, I've never had any before last night. It wasn't like I was completely drunk. More like a little tipsy, I would say. I have nothing to go off of there, as to what is what, but I've read about responses and bodily reactions, and that's what I think happened.

But, along with that, if a person drinks too much, it's actually harder to have an orgasm. This is the body's natural biological response to inebriation. I've learned this in school, somewhat. Not in extreme detail, but we discussed it to some degree, and that's what happens.

Which is... odd...

I've never had an orgasm when I wasn't drunk, and yet Ethan gave me multiple orgasms while we were both drunk? Sort of drunk. A little tipsy. Definitely buzzed.

Except we had sex for hours, and alcohol doesn't stay in your system for *that* long, especially the small few drinks we had, so...

It doesn't make sense. This is like trying to divide by zero. My mental calculator can't compute this equation. Realistically, I don't think this should have happened, but obviously it did, so...

The next logical conclusion is to wonder what would happen when we're both completely sober?

What am I even doing? What am I thinking? Why am I finished eating? Why am I putting my plates in the sink? Why am I walking down the hall and heading upstairs?

To go take a shower. Yes, that's it.

Then why am I going towards Ethan's room instead of mine? I stop outside the door and listen to the sound of him showering. I can't exactly hear him, but I can hear the water, can sort of hear it splashing against his body, and he must be naked.

He was naked last night. We both were. And this morning, too.

I put my hand on the doorknob. Just resting it there. Just in case. I'm not going to open the door. I won't.

Our parents won't be back for a week, though, right?

# 15 - Ethan

YEAH, WELL, what the fuck was I thinking? Why would I tell Ashley we could do a friends with benefits relationship for a week while our parents are away? Fuck if I know.

First off, I wasn't thinking with my brain, I was thinking with my cock. There's no other way to explain that, and I'm not even going to bother.

Speaking of...

Water cascades down my muscled body, splashing onto my feet while I stand here, entranced, in the shower. My cock is hard, and it's really fucking hungry. Hungry for her. God, I don't even know what she's doing to me. This can't be good. I can't stop thinking about her.

I remember all of it, or I think I do. I remember sinking into her, the feeling of her tight pussy clamping onto my throbbing cock. I remember the look of pained ecstasy on her face when she bursts, her orgasm overcoming her. I remember how she kicked and thrashed beneath me, spasming uncontrollably. Then she started laughing, giddy, a pleasure overload.

I remember it and I want to see it again.

It's not going to happen, though. She's not going to come up here. Yeah, well, it was a mistake, and it's going to stay a mistake. Friends with benefits? Hah! Seriously, what the fuck?

Ashley is my sister now. Stepsister. Whatever. Doesn't matter. Same thing. I shouldn't be trying to fuck her, I should be trying to help her get over this stupid fuck who dumped her.

That's the thing, though. I'm not good at this relationship shit. Or I'm really good depending on how you look at it. I know I can't give these girls what they always want in the long term, and I know it won't last between us. It's not a big deal and I don't really care that much, but I like showing them what they should look for in a guy, too. I like showing them that they shouldn't compromise, that they should be able to have explosive sex, that orgasms are really fucking nice, and that yeah, guys exist that want to pamper the fuck out of them.

So that's what I do. Explosive sex, as many orgasms as they can handle--sometimes even more than that, since I'm a real people pleaser here--and I treat them like the princess every guy should see them as. It's nice. I'm doing a public service here, making the world a better place, one orgasm at a time.

For a week or so. That's it. That's enough.

I'm not saying I'm some golden child wonder boy here. I'm still a cocky, selfish asshole. I take a lot of pleasure in watching their pleasure-riddled bodies squirming beneath me. It's a give and take situation, you know? I give, and then I take. It's not hard to understand. Yeah, maybe some good comes out of it, maybe they go on to find a better guy. Someone not like me, but someone like me, too. Someone who won't stop answering their calls after a week, and someone who won't randomly text them a month or two later to see if they're up for a booty call.

That's the difference between a bad boy and a good guy. A bad boy treats a girl like a princess for a week, then finds another one. A good guy treats a girl like a princess for the rest of his life.

I'm not doing that. I don't have time for that. It's too much to ask. I have other shit to do.

Like...

Holy fucking shit, she just walked in.

Before this, I was seriously considering rubbing one out. Just grabbing my cock, stroking hard, watching my cum splash against the shower wall, mixing with the falling water from the showerhead. I don't do that often; never really have the need, especially considering there's a girl around any corner just waiting to do it for me. But, yeah, fuck, Ashley, I can't stop thinking about her. I don't know why. I'm fucked up, alright? There, I said it.

Maybe she's fucked up, too, because she's standing there, naked, leaning against my bathroom door, staring at me. Shy. Cute and coy as fuck. God, I want to slam her against my bed and rail the fuck out of her. Just pound away like there's no tomorrow. What's she even doing here?

I know what she's doing here. Yeah, she's standing to the side, kind of looking away, still refusing to accept it, but that goddamn fucking twinkle in her eyes gives her away.

She wants this. She wants me. Inside her. My cock showing her exactly what real pleasure is.

That's what she wants? Yeah, I can do that for her. Give and take, right?

# A NOTE FROM MIA

A NOTE FROM ME, YAY!

I don't actually have a lot to say here, so I'm going to keep it short, sweet, and simple. I just wanted to tell you a little bit of what's going on with this series.

First, the series is done! Everything will be available and published in short order. This is my first book, and I'm really excited about it, so I'm trying to do the best I can with everything. This is a lot different from anything I've ever done, but it's fun and a neat learning experience.

Second, I know that cliffhangers aren't always the most fun, and I'm sorry for that. Doing it this way gave me more of a chance to make sure everything was good and as perfect as I can make it, though. Just know that everything is all finished, still, so you won't have to wait and can keep reading right now if you want. The e-book versions are a little more affordable, so if you'd like to get those, I would highly recommend it!

Also, I wanted to leave room for more, just in case. The series does end, but maybe you'll want more? I know I would possibly like to write more, and I have some fun ideas for it, but who knows?

I like bad boys and good girls either way, though, so that's what you can expect from me. With a forbidden lovers and Romeo and Juliet twist, for added fun and excitement. Also some romantic comedy, because who doesn't like to laugh? I think steamy scenes and laughing go together like peanut butter and chocolate. Yeah, I mean, they can be serious if you want, and that's sexy and fun sometimes, but laughing and playing while being intimate is... rawr! I love it!

So this is me, Mia. And that's what you can expect from me, too. Let's be friends and see how it goes.

Oh, and I wanted to thank Cerys (du Lys) for helping me with editing and making me these gorgeous covers. She's the best. Thank you to Ethan (Winters), too, for letting me name my character after him and for helping me with making my bad boy sexy and fun. Ethan is fun, and also kind of sexy, so it works. Don't tell him I said that, though! He'll get an ego.

If you'd like to see more from all of us, we have a nice webpage set up to showcase our works that you can check out. Here is a link:

Cherrylily.com

I hope you liked Ashley and Ethan's story so far, and I hope you'll keep reading. There's plenty more where that came from, and I'm excited about it!

If you did like it, I would love love love if you could leave a review, too! It's a really nice thing to do, and I appreciate it. Tell me what you thought of Ashley and Ethan, and let me know if you liked their silly sexy flirty back and forth I hate you I love you kinds of conversations, haha. It gets more fun the more you read, too.

Thanks so much for reading my book!

~Mia

# ABOUT THE AUTHOR

Mia likes to have fun in all aspects of her life. Whether she's out enjoying the beautiful weather or spending time at home reading a book, a smile is never far from her face. She's prone to randomly laughing at nothing in particular except for whatever idea amuses her at any given moment.

Sometimes you just need to enjoy life, right?

She loves to read, dance, and explore outdoors. Chamomile tea and bubble baths are two of her favorite things. Flowers are especially nice, and she could get lost in a garden if it's big enough and no one's around to remind her that there are other things to do.

She lives in New Hampshire, where the weather is beautiful and the autumn colors are amazing.

Manufactured by Amazon.ca
Bolton, ON